Growing

# CHATTER-BOX JAMIE

Nancy Evans Cooney

illustrated by
Marylin Hafner

G. P. Putnam's Sons • New York

G. P. Putnam's Sons, a division of The Putnam & Grosset Group,
200 Madison Avenue, New York, NY 10016.
Published simultaneously in Canada.
Printed in Hong Kong by South China Printing Co. (1988) Ltd.
Text set in Goudy Old Style.

Library of Congress Cataloging-in-Publication Data
Cooney, Nancy Evans. Chatterbox Jamie / by Nancy Evans Cooney ;
illustrated by Marylin Hafner.   p. cm.
Summary: Jamie enjoys all the activities at his nursery school but
does not talk until just the right time for him.
[1. Nursery schools—Fiction.   2. Schools—Fiction.   3. Mutism,
Elective—Fiction.] I. Hafner, Marylin, ill. II. Title.
PZ7.C7843Ch  1993[E]—dc20  92-11001  CIP  AC
ISBN 0-399-22208-1
1  3  5  7  9  10  8  6  4  2
First Impression

For Jim and Sherley —NEC

For Jamie Holton —MH

Jamie was starting nursery school next week. He danced around Mom and Amy, full of questions.

"What is it like?" he asked.

"Remember the big playroom we visited? The paint corner, the blocks and games, the place to play house…"

"Who will play?" he interrupted.

"Kristen and Bobby and David…"

"But I don't know them."

"Not yet," his mom said, smiling, "but you will soon."

Later, Jamie asked, "Do I go tomorrow?"
"No, not tomorrow."

When Dad came home, Jamie told him about the blocks so big he could stand on them.

Dad laughed. "Every night you tell me something about school and you haven't even started yet. You're a regular chatterbox."

"Do I go tomorrow?"

"No, not yet."

One morning, Dad announced, "Today's the day."

All the way to nursery school, Jamie and Dad talked. They sang one of their silly songs about goldfish swimming in their pockets, and suddenly they were there.

Then Dad stooped down, hugged Jamie, and said, "I'll be back to get you at lunchtime. Have fun." Off he went, leaving Jamie alone.

Alone!

It didn't matter that other boys and girls were playing in the room.

It didn't matter that Mrs. Romano walked beside him and told him the names of the children.

It didn't matter that her helper, Miss Bonner, smiled at him.

Jamie was alone with no Dad or Mom.

Mrs. Romano asked, "Do you want to play house? Kristen is cooking and Jack is sweeping."

But Jamie stood still like a robot with its power turned off; no words came.

Two boys were rolling out Play-Doh at a small table.
"You can have the green," said Peter.
But Jamie didn't say a word.

At snack time, he did as the others did. He washed his hands and ate his crackers and cheese and drank his juice. David sat beside him. "Orange juice is my favorite." But Jamie just nodded.

Outside, Bobby waved from the top of the slide. David and some others were building a sand castle.

Kristen called from the jungle gym, "I'm the highest!"

But Jamie just stood there and watched.

Later when they had their circle time, he listened while
Mrs. Romano read a story about a squirrel, and then they
all sang together.

All except Jamie.

When his dad came back, Jamie ran straight to him.
  "Dad, guess who was there—Bobby and David and Kristen
and Mrs. Romano…"

He bounced on the car seat. "And guess what we had for snack time—cheese and juice and crackers....And they had Play-Doh and a jungle gym and..."

"Whoa!" Dad laughed. "You can't tell me everything at once."

But Jamie didn't tell that he hadn't talked.

The next school day, Jamie played with the other children.
He scampered up the climbing dome and went high on
the swing.

Kristen painted at the easel. "I'm making a picture for my baby brother," she said.

So Jamie drew a picture of a bird for Amy.
But he still didn't say a word.

When David said, "Want to build a bridge?" Jamie helped
pile up the big blocks.

But he didn't say anything.

Twice a week, Jamie went to nursery school. He chattered all the way there and all the way back.

At home, he told Mom all about his day while she fed Amy. But he didn't tell that he hadn't talked.

One evening, after Amy had had her bath and she lay in her crib, cooing, Jamie whispered to her, "I don't know why I can't talk at school. My mouth just won't work."

Amy grabbed his finger and clutched it tight.

Jamie felt a little better.

The weather got colder and Jamie had to wear his heavy jacket.

Then one day, Kristen's mother visited nursery school with her baby boy. It was Kristen's birthday and her mother brought cupcakes to share at snack time.

Jamie edged close to the baby's side.

He put his finger near the baby's hand. The baby grabbed hold and wouldn't let go.

Jamie burst out, "I have a baby, too! She's my sister and her name is Amy."

Mrs. Romano came to him with a big smile. As they walked toward the carpet for circle time, Jamie chattered about Amy, about his favorite juice, and about what story he liked best.

"I like to sing, too," he said. "I know a silly song about goldfish swimming in my pockets. Want to hear it?"

Mrs. Romano laughed and said, "Yes. Sing it for all of us." And he did.